53/

D0037140

lov•   ere!

Every child learns to read in a different way and at his or her own speed. You can help your young reader improve and become more confident by encouraging his or her own interests and abilities. You can also guide your child's spiritual development by reading stories with biblical values and Bible stories, like I Can Read! books published by Zonderkidz. From books your child reads with you to the first books he or she reads alone, there are I Can Read! books for every stage of reading:

DISCARD

SHARED READING
Basic language, word repetition, and whimsical illustrations, ideal for sharing with your emergent reader.

BEGINNING READING
Short sentences, familiar words, and simple concepts for children eager to read on their own.

READING WITH HELP
Engaging stories, longer sentences, and language play for developing readers.

READING ALONE
Complex plots, challenging vocabulary, and high-interest topics for the independent reader.

ADVANCED READING
Short paragraphs, chapters, and exciting themes for the perfect bridge to chapter books.

I Can Read! books have introduced children to the joy of reading since 1957. Featuring award-winning authors and illustrators and a fabulous cast of beloved characters, I Can Read! books set the standard for beginning readers.

A lifetime of discovery begins with the magical words **"I Can Read!"**

Visit www.icanread.com for information on enriching your child's reading experience.
Visit www.zonderkidz.com for more Zonderkidz I Can Read! titles.

I sought the Lord, and he answered me;
he delivered me from all my fears.
—Psalm 34:4

ZONDERKIDZ

The Berenstain Bears® Do Not Fear, God is Near
Copyright© 2013 by Berenstain Publishing, Inc.
Illustrations © 2013 by Berenstain Publishing, Inc.

Requests for information should be addressed to:

Zonderkidz, 5300 Patterson Ave SE, Grand Rapids, Michigan 49530

ISBN 978-0-310-72511-4

Editor: Mary Hassinger
Design: Diane Mielke

Printed in China

13 14 15 16 17 18 /DSC/ 10 9 8 7 6 5 4 3 2 1

ZONDERkidz | I Can Read! | BEGINNING READING 1

The Berenstain Bears.
Do Not Fear, God is Near

Story and Pictures By
Stan & Jan Berenstain with Mike Berenstain

Living Lights™

ZONDERVAN.com/
AUTHORTRACKER
follow your favorite authors

When Sister Bear was little
she was afraid of lots of things.

She was afraid of bugs.

She was afraid of birds.

She was afraid of dogs

and thunder and
lightning.

But Sister was most afraid
of spooky shadows.

When Sister got bigger
she understood that trust in God
takes away our fears.

As the Bible says:
"When I am afraid, I put my trust in you.
In God, whose word I praise—
in God I trust and am not afraid."

She was not even afraid
of thunder and lightning!

But Sister was still afraid of spooky shadows.

"You know, Sister," Mama told her, "God is always near you, even when things seem scary."

Brother Bear thought Sister was silly.

He teased her.

"Scaredy bear! Scaredy bear!

Afraid of your own shadow,"

Brother teased.

It was not nice.

But big brothers are not always

nice to little sisters—even Brother Bear.

"That is not nice," said Mama.

"You should be kind to your sister.

As the Good Book says,

'Anyone who withholds kindness

from a friend forsakes the fear

of the Almighty.'"

"That is right," said Papa.

"Besides, Sister is brave about

many other things."

Sister was not afraid of frogs and toads.

She was not afraid of spooky-shaped trees.

And one day when a big spider
came and sat beside her ...

Sister scared the spider away.

BOO!

But Sister was still scared
of shadows.
She forgot that the Bible says,
"Do not be afraid or discouraged,
for the Lord God, my God, is with you."

"Help!" Sister cried.

"Spooky shadows!"

Sister ran into the tree house
and into Papa's arms.

"We must do something,"
said Mama.

"I have an idea," said Papa.

"Look, Sister," Papa said.
"Shadows can be fun."
He gave her a flashlight
to shine on the wall.

Then Papa made a funny

shadow.

"It looks like a bird,"

said Sister.

Sister looked at Papa's hands.

She looked at the shadow.

Papa wiggled his hands.

The bird flapped its wings.

"It is flapping its wings!" said Sister.

"May I try?"

Papa held the flashlight.

Sister made a bird shadow too.

"You see," said Papa, "a shadow is what happens when something gets in the way of a light."

Then Papa showed Sister
how to make a shadow rabbit,

a shadow goose,

and a shadow dog.

Later that night, Sister played
a trick on Brother.

She made a big shadow bird
and flapped its wings.

"Yipe!" Brother cried.
"A spooky shadow!"

Sister knew she should not tease.
But she wanted to teach
Brother a little lesson.

When they were in bed,

Sister knew she should be kind to Brother.

But she teased him

one more time.

She made a rabbit,
a goose, and a dog.
"Spooky shadows!"
Brother cried.

Papa came in.

"You should not tease your brother,"
he said.

"But I see you are not afraid
of shadows anymore."

"I guess not,"
Sister said.

But Brother was—a little.

Then he remembered that God

was watching over him.

As the Book of Proverbs says,

"When you lie down, you will not be afraid;

When you lie down, your sleep will be sweet.